MY DADDY SLAYS DRAGONS

Written by Stephanie Kahle   Illustrated by Karen Riedler

Fulton Books, Inc.
Meadville, PA

First originally published by Fulton Books 2020

ISBN 978-1-64654-220-8 (Paperback)
ISBN 978-1-64654-223-9 (Hardcover)
ISBN 978-1-64654-222-2 (Digital)

Printed in the United States of America

Burn Institute.®

Doing our part to help heal those who have been affected by fire. Ten percent of the proceeds of this book go toward teaching children fire safety, installing fire alarms in the homes of elderly and by empowering burn victims.

Learn more at:
BurnInstitute.org

My Daddy slays dragons,
just like in the days of old.
He's a knight in shining armor,
like in the stories I've been told.

Whenever duty calls
on a steel horse he rides,
the fight can last for weeks
or till the danger subsides.

My Mommy's a fair maiden,
buried in laundry and toys.
She doesn't tend to dwarfs,
just us little girls and boys.

Just like all the other heroes,
he must be brave and true.
Daddy says it always helps
to have a real good crew!

He joins other dragon slayers,
some he might befriend.
They have to work together
so the dragon meets his end.

Sometimes they go to forests
in kingdoms far away.
He keeps my picture close,
longing to come home and play.

I worry about my Daddy.
A fierce battle he will fight.
Mom says he'll be too busy
to call and say good night.

I know Daddy's thinking of me
and the work I have to do.
Keeping everyone safe in our castle
is an important job too!

Someday I'll conquer dragons,
and we'll never be apart.
For now I stay with Mommy.
Here's where he leaves his heart.

And when the battle's over
and the heroes do prevail,
I can't wait to hear my Daddy
tell his adventurous tale!

He'll walk through our front door.
The scent of smoke will fill the air.
We'll all give him hugs,
and he'll kiss his lady fair.

She'll add his armor to the laundry,
and he'll clean up all his gear.
Everything will be ready
for the next time danger is near.

My daddy slays dragons.
He's a hero, I've been told.
He's a knight in shining armor,
just like in the days of old.

FIRE SAFETY TIPS FOR KIDS

1. Never play with matches or lighters.
2. Crawl low under smoke during a fire.
3. Call 9-1-1 if there is an emergency.
4. Have a family meeting place in case of a home fire.
5. Stop, Drop, and Roll if your clothes catch on fire.
6. Cool a burn with cool water.

Burn Institute®

ABOUT THE AUTHOR

Stephanie Kahle works in education at Ramona Unified School District. She has an Associate of Arts degree in Early Childhood Education and a Bachelor of Arts degree in Sociology. She wrote this book in 2008 while her husband was deployed on a strike team for twenty-one days to combat the wildfires that ravaged the state of California. She was home with two toddlers and wished for a book she could read to her children, explaining why their dad was gone for so long. She lives in Southern California with her husband of more than twenty years, Fire Captain Ehren, their two children, Tehren and Vailyn, and a couple of sweet pups.

About the Illustrator

A graduate of electronic art from Chico State, Karen Riedler is a creative adventurer. She loves to play with concepts of fantasy and surrealism. Her main passion is for illustration, fashion, and painting. She has two self-published books under her belt titled *Ordinary Monsters* and *Darby*. Karen involves herself in her community by painting murals and participating in regular creative projects. She is thrilled to have worked on this book as she relished the opportunity to give back to the firefighters that saved her family's home. She lives east of San Diego with her husband, Cory, her daughter, Luna and a new baby boy on the way. To see more of Karen's work, check out StudioRiedler.com.

CPSIA information can be obtained
at www.ICGtesting.com
Printed in the USA
LVHW070019200322
713895LV00002B/3